I breathed a sigh of relief and settled down in my new home – Lizzy's lovely thick hair. I felt sorry for Gregory, of course – about to have his head flushed down the toilet by Duncan – but what could I do? I was just a head-louse, after all . . .

Also available by John Dougherty,
and published by Young Corgi Books:

ZEUS ON THE LOOSE
'Energetic and page-turning' *INK magazine*

For more information about John Dougherty:
www.visitingauthor.com

"Niteracy" hour

John Dougherty

Illustrated by Georgien Overwater

YOUNG CORGI

NITERACY HOUR
A YOUNG CORGI BOOK 0552 550825

First publication in Great Britain

Young Corgi edition published 2005

1 3 5 7 9 10 8 6 4 2

Set in Bembo MT Schlbk

Young Corgi Books are published by Random House Children's Books,
61–63 Uxbridge Road, London W5 5SA,
a division of The Random House Group Ltd,
in Australia by Random House Australia (Pty) Ltd,
20 Alfred Street, Milsons Point, Sydney, NSW 2061, Australia,
in New Zealand by Random House New Zealand Ltd,
18 Poland Road, Glenfield, Auckland 10, New Zealand,
and in South Africa by Random House (Pty) Ltd,
Endulini, 5A Jubilee Road, Parktown 2193, South Africa

THE RANDOM HOUSE GROUP Limited Reg. No. 954009
www.**kids**at**randomhouse**.co.uk

A CIP catalogue record for this book is available from the British Library.

Printed and bound in Great Britain by
Cox & Wyman Ltd, Reading, Berkshire.

Contents

Chapter One

A Lousy Start

Before we start, let's get one thing straight. A nit is an empty egg, OK? So don't call me a nit.

I'm a head-louse.

Please, don't go "Eeeeugh!". I can't *stand* some of the noises you human children make, and "Eeeeugh!" is one of the worst.

So, anyway, I'm a head-louse. But I'm
not an ordinary head-louse. And this is my
story.

I hatched out on the head of a small
human while his teacher was taking the
register. Just before she got to his name, in
fact, which turned out to be Gregory. Out
I popped and had a look round.

Mmmm, I thought. Lovely clean hair.
Nice!

I was hungry, so I got out my little mouth-parts and had something to eat.

What did I eat? I ate Gregory, of course.

No, don't be daft, I didn't eat him *all*. I wouldn't have room. I just sucked some of his blood. Not very much. He didn't even notice.

I'd just finished my breakfast when the teacher started the first lesson. And this is where I turned out to be different from any other head-louse.

I listened.

What I didn't know then – having only just been hatched – is that most head-lice *don't* listen. To be honest, they're generally a bit thick.

But *I* listened.

I found out later that Gregory was by far the best listener in the class. Better even than his teacher, Mrs Campbell. And the only thing I can think of is – well, you know how, when a human is really good at something, people say 'it's in their blood'? I think good listening was in Gregory's blood. And when I sucked his blood, it got into mine, too.

So I became a really good listener.

Wow! What a way to start life! It was amazing! It was fantastic! It was incredible!

It was . . . story time!

Actually, Mrs Campbell didn't call it story time. She called it 'Literacy Hour'. What she was doing was reading out bits of stories for the children to compare. And every single bit of story she read out was. . . mind-blowing. Hearing them was like being hatched again into some astonishing, marvellous, brave new world.

 My favourite was from a book called *Treasure Island*, by Robert Louis Stevenson. It's about a boy called Jim Hawkins, who leaves his

home and his ordinary life and sails away
to adventure on the high seas. As I listened
I could almost hear the waves foaming
and thundering against those far-off
shores.

I was sorry when that bit of the lesson came to an end and the children were set to work, writing about the differences between the stories. I didn't care how they were different; I just wanted to hear more and more. I especially wanted to find out what happened to Jim Hawkins in *Treasure Island*.

But Mrs Campbell stopped reading, and all the children started writing. So I just sat and listened to what was going on in the class.

Some of which wasn't very nice at all.

I don't mean the lesson; I mean what some of the other children were saying to each other when they should have been working. There was one big kid called Duncan who kept saying all kinds of nasty stuff about who he was going to 'get' at playtime, and what he was going to do to them.

I didn't like Duncan.

It turned out Duncan didn't like
Gregory, either.

At playtime, I was really enjoying being
outdoors for the first time ever. I could
hear the birds singing in the trees, and the
swish of the leaves in the gentle wind. The
sounds of the children playing and the
traffic rumbling past the school were . . .
magic. Really beautiful. All
these sounds that I'd never
heard before! I rode
around on Gregory's
head, clinging to one
of his hairs, just
loving the sounds
and the feeling
of being alive
and newly-
hatched, with my
whole life in front
of me.

Tally ho!

Then the world shook.

Well, that's what it felt like. In fact, it wasn't the world that was shaking; it was Gregory's head. And the reason Gregory's head was shaking was that Duncan had grabbed him by the throat and was shoving him up against the playground wall.

Then he said, "Listen, Eggy Greggy, if you *ever* tell on me again, I'm going to stick your head down the toilet and pull the chain, all right?"

I held on tight and peeked out from the jungle of Gregory's hair. Imagine a giant with huge nostrils, great big jagged teeth and an enormous pink slug for a tongue. That's what Duncan looked like to me. I'm only little, compared to people, so he looked *enormous*. Enormous and ugly.

Gregory nodded – which made me feel a little seasick – and said he understood, and Duncan let him go.

But of course the first thing that Gregory did when playtime was over was to go to Mrs Campbell and tell her that Duncan had pushed him up against a wall and threatened to stick his head down the toilet.

So Duncan got in trouble with Mrs Campbell – and he wasn't very happy about it. He spent the rest of the next lesson glaring at Gregory and making toilet-flushing gestures with his hands.

Gregory didn't seem to be very worried – but I was.

Because if Gregory was going to have his head flushed down the toilet, then the last place I wanted to be was on that head.

Which is just where I was – with no way of getting off.

Chapter Two

Lousy Luck

I was getting frantic. It was nearly lunchtime. When the class went to dinner, Gregory was going to have his head flushed down the toilet; and since I was on his head, I was going to be washed out to sea. At least, I might be. I'd seen the toilet, and I really didn't know if I could hold on to Gregory's hair in there.

I'd have loved to go to sea – but in a magnificent tall sailing ship, like Jim Hawkins, not just flushed away on a piece of soggy toilet-paper with no wonderful stories to listen to.

Then I had a real piece of luck.

Paired reading.

For the ten minutes before lunch, Mrs Campbell asked everyone to sit in twos and read to each other in their quietest voices.

"And I mean *quietest*!" she said. "Especially you, William!" Gregory's friend, William, was the noisiest boy in the class, always talking.

Gregory went to sit beside Lizzy.

First she read to him, in a really really quiet voice, which wasn't a problem because Gregory was an extremely good listener. Amazingly, fantastically good.

Then he read to her, in a really really quiet voice; and that *was* a problem, because Lizzy wasn't such a good listener. Not at all. But after Mrs Campbell had looked at her a couple of times and said, "Lizzy, are you *listening* to your partner?" she stopped fidgeting – quite so much – and stopped looking around – kind of – and tried really hard.

The problem was, she couldn't really hear what Gregory was saying, because his quietest reading voice was really, really, *really* quiet and she wasn't very good at listening. Besides, William was at the next table, reading out loud *very* loudly – and talking lots as usual, too.

Lizzy leaned in towards Gregory, to hear what he was saying. But she *still* couldn't hear him. So she leaned in even further. And her head touched his.

I saw my chance. I crawled across Gregory's head, to where his hair met  Lizzy's, and carefully picked my way across. It was a bit scary, because I didn't know if Lizzy was going to pull her head away when I was half-way over. Step by step I went, as Gregory read quietly and steadily below my feet.

Finally I was there.

I breathed a sigh of relief and settled down in my new home – Lizzy's lovely thick hair. I felt sorry for Gregory, of course – about to have his head flushed down the toilet by Duncan – but what could I do? I was just a head-louse, after all.

All that worry had left me feeling very hungry, so I settled down for a nice long lunch. Lizzy tasted delicious!

Don't go "Eeeeugh!". I didn't go "Eeeeugh!" when I sat on Lizzy's head in the dinner hall and watched a hundred and fifty kids eating *their* lunch. Now *that* was disgusting.

After lunch, we went out into the playground.

And Lizzy ran.

Whoooo-eee! It was *such* fun. I can't begin to describe it! It was better than the best roller-coaster you've ever been on. Because Lizzy was the fastest runner, the best footballer, the highest high-jumper, the whirliest cartwheeler in the class – maybe even the whole school. She was an absolute red-hot bundle of energy. No wonder she couldn't keep still in lessons!

As soon as she got out into the playground, Lizzy was off – faster than a rocket, zippier than a racing car. I held on tight, feeling the wind whip past and watching the world blur. It was brilliant!

She didn't keep still all lunchtime. She chased people, she scored goals, she somersaulted and cartwheeled and leaped and jumped and hurdled! I loved every minute of it.

Well, almost. There were two bits of playtime that I didn't like.

The first was when William ran up and said excitedly, "Lizzy! Lizzy! Did you hear? Duncan put Gregory's head down the loo!" I felt sad, hearing that. I could tell that Lizzy did, too.

"Someone ought to do something about Duncan," she said angrily.

"Yeah, but what?" William answered. "Gregory's the only person who's ever been brave enough to tell on him – and look where that got him!"

The second bit of playtime that I didn't like was when Duncan stuck out his foot and tripped Lizzy. Then  he ran off, laughing nastily. When Lizzy picked herself up, her knee was bleeding.

"Someone *seriously* ought to do something about him," she muttered.

I felt really bad for her.

I felt sorry for Gregory, too, when he came in with wet hair and a drowned expression. I expected him to go and tell Mrs Campbell straight away, but instead he just sat miserably down beside William.

What could I do? I was only a head-louse. If a great big human child was going to give up, then there wasn't much hope that I could do anything, was there?

As Lizzy was sitting fairly still now and not likely to do much running until home-time, I decided to explore.

Lizzy's hair, I decided, was a really nice place to live. It smelt lovely and shampooey, and it was all warm and cosy. And then there was the sheer fun of  being there when Lizzy ran. I couldn't imagine why there wasn't a whole village of head-lice living there.

Those were the sort of thoughts I was thinking to myself as I crawled along the top of Lizzy's head, through all the lovely thick hair. I made my way to the back of her head and started to crawl down, pushing aside strands of hair as if they were long, long grass and I was a jungle explorer.

Suddenly, I heard a terrible sound. It was faint and distant at first, but as I continued down the back of Lizzy's head it grew louder.

It was a voice – but not a human voice. It was coming from somewhere on Lizzy's head, not far away. And it was howling – a wild, painful howl.

"Doom!" it wailed. "DOOOM!"

Chapter Three

A Lousy Conversation

My first thought was to
hide, deep in Lizzy's
hair, close to the skin.
But the horrible sound
didn't stop.

"Doom!" it went. "Doom!
Death! A vile punishment on us all!"

Then I realized something. Not only
was the voice not a human voice – it
wasn't speaking in a human language. It
was speaking louse-speak. That made me
feel braver. If there'd been a wolf or a
jaguar or something hiding in Lizzy's hair,
that would have been really scary, but I
felt fairly sure wolves and jaguars couldn't
speak louse-speak.

I know now that wolves and jaguars don't live on people's heads either, but I didn't know that then. I'd only been hatched that morning, after all; and I'd only heard about wolves and jaguars in Mrs Campbell's Literacy Hour stories.

I followed the sound, carefully pushing strands of hair aside as I went. The wailing and howling got louder and louder, and finally – sensing I was really close now – I climbed up a hair to see if I could see where it was coming from.

It was a louse. The first other
head-louse I'd ever seen. He
was pushing his way
through Lizzy's hair, not
far off, and he didn't
look dangerous; just
slightly bonkers. A bit
like Ben Gunn in
Treasure Island. He's
a pirate who gets
marooned by the
other pirates all by
himself on a desert
island for years, and
he goes mad
through loneliness.
Mrs Campbell had
read out a bit about
him that morning, too.
I climbed down again and
approached the other louse, a
little shyly.

"Um . . . hello," I said.

The louse turned slowly towards me, a wild expression on his face.

"Flee!" he howled.

"I'm not a flea," I told him, slightly offended. "I'm a head-louse. Just like you."

He rolled his eyes crazily. "Beware!" he moaned. "BEWARE!"

"Er . . . beware what?" I asked.

"Your doom! Beware your doom! DOO-OOM!"

This really wasn't terribly helpful.

"What . . . what *sort* of doom would

24

that be, exactly?" I asked him. "Only, you see, I'm new round here . . . well, I'm just plain new, actually – hatched this morning – and I haven't seen any dooms. I'm not sure I've got one, to be honest."

The other louse rolled his eyes at me again.

"It comes in the night – just before the lights go out!" he groaned. "A monster! A terrible monster, with horrible sharp teeth! Swifter than a louse can crawl, more silent than the darkness! It comes with no warning, hears no pleading, offers no mercy! They call it . . . *the Comb!* And it is disaster, death, DOOM!"

"Gosh!" I said. "That sounds scary! But I guess you escaped from it. I mean, you're not dead or anything . . ." My voice tailed off under his frenzied glare.

"Yes, *I* escaped!" he whispered madly. "I alone escaped the terrible doom! Doom, I say! DOO-OOM!" He lowered his voice, so that I had to lean uncomfortably close to hear him. "I have a hiding place!" he muttered "Yes, a *secret* hiding place! Where the Comb never comes! I hide there, I do, and it never finds me!"

"Where?" I asked curiously.

He looked sharply and suspiciously at me. "No!" he hissed angrily. "No! It's mine! It's not yours! Never, never! *My* hiding place! No room for two!"

"OK, OK, I was only asking!" I grumbled. I felt a bit sorry for this mad old louse, stuck here on his own for goodness knows how long, but I didn't think that was any excuse for being rude.

I was beginning to worry a little, too. What was I going to do that night, when the Comb came, if he didn't let me hide with him?

Then I heard something that would have chilled me to the bone, if head-lice had bones to chill.

It was Mrs Campbell's voice.

"Lizzy!" she said. "Just look at the state of you! Has your hair been like that since lunchtime? Off you go to the cloakrooms and drag a comb through your hair, now! Every inch of it!"

I felt the world shake under me as Lizzy stood up.

"The Comb!" I yelped in panic.

The effect on the mad old louse was immediate.

"FLEE!!!" he yelled. Before I could do anything, he turned and disappeared into the thickness of Lizzy's hair.

"Take me with you! Hide me!" I pleaded, shouting after him, but he was gone. I heard his voice, fading into the distance – "Dooom! DOO-OOMMM!!!" – and then I was alone.

Suddenly the horror of it all was too much for me. With a cry, I turned and ran. I felt as if the Comb was already chasing me, hunting me down through the long thick glossy hair. I ran as I'd never run before, desperate to escape Lizzy's head, frantic to find safety on some other human. Up over the crown of her head I raced, across the top of her scalp, towards the place where no more hair grew.

There was no time to stop; her forehead appeared like the sheer deadly drop of a rocky cliff.

With a desperate strength, I leaped.

The classroom air whistled past my head as I rose into the cool silence. It seemed to whisper to me: *Head-lice can't do this!* It was true, I was sure of it. Head-lice couldn't run, and we couldn't jump. Why could I?

And then I had a horrible thought: I hadn't looked before I leaped.

I was hurtling through the air with no way of stopping, and no way of turning. I was going to splat against the wall, or I was going to fall into the sink. I was going to crash, or I was going to drown.

Either way, I was going to die.

Chapter Four

A Louse Up

As I soared over the heads of the children, my whole life flashed in front of my eyes.

Of course, that took less than two seconds. I'd only been hatched that morning.

Then there was nothing but the wide wall and the watery sink, both rushing to meet me. Both eager to end my short life.

But as I passed over the very last table, a miracle happened.

William stood up.

Thwack! Into his soft, curly hair I shot, landing so hard that little lights flashed inside my eyes. I lay there, panting and dizzy, clinging to a strand of hair, waiting until William sat down and the ceiling high above me stopped looping and swirling and spinning.

When it finally felt safe to move again, I carefully made my way down through William's hair to his scalp, just above  his left ear. I got out my little mouth-parts again and had a feed.

"Oh, boy!" I said to myself. "I needed that!"

I felt William's head move under me as he looked up.

"What?" he said, turning round.

I froze. William couldn't have heard me, could he?

"I didn't say anything," Gregory said.

"Oh," said William, "I thought somebody said something."

"Someone did," Gregory said. "It was you."

They went back to their work, and I

realized how daft I was being. After all, louse-speak is very quiet – and it doesn't sound anything like human language. William couldn't possibly have heard me. The more I thought about it, the more ridiculous I felt. I almost laughed out loud.

"You're so silly!" I told myself.

"No I'm not!" William burst out, looking up again.

I froze once more, silenced by surprise.

"Not what?" said Gregory.

"I'm not silly!" William said.

"I never said you were," Gregory answered.

"Yes you did!" William retorted angrily. "I heard you!"

Gregory shook his head. "I didn't say anything," he said.

"Why are you telling lies?" William squeaked indignantly.

"Gregory doesn't tell lies, William!" said Lizzy, passing by the table on her way back from the cloakroom. "Everyone knows that!"

"*You're* lying *too!*" William said furiously, his voice rising. He sounded near to tears now.

"They're *not* lying!" I said without thinking.

Now it was William's turn to freeze. He looked from Gregory to Lizzy, and back again. It was obvious to me now that he *could* hear me; and it was clear to him that it was neither Gregory's nor Lizzy's voice that he'd heard. Trembling slightly, he put his hand up.

"Um . . . miss," he said in an unusually small voice, "can I go and get a drink? I don't feel well."

As we passed Duncan's table, the big bully grinned nastily.

"You're going mad, William!" he hissed. "Only mad people hear voices!"

Out we went to the toilets, where a drinking fountain stood next to a big mirror.

"Don't worry, William," I said. "You weren't hearing things."

William looked up, and all around, startled.

"Who said that?" he demanded.

"I did," I told him.

"Yeah, but . . . but . . . who *are* you? *Where* are you? Why can't I see you?"

"I haven't really got a name," I said. "And you can't see me because I'm very small. But I'm a bit afraid to tell you where I am."

"Don't be afraid!" he said. "I won't hurt you!"

"Do you promise?" I said.

He crossed his heart. "Promise!" he said. "Double promise!"

"OK," I said. "I'm on your head. Just above your left ear."

I could see his face in the big mirror. He looked puzzled.

"What are you doing there?" he asked.

"Well . . ." I said hesitantly, "don't forget
– you promised not to hurt me. I'm on
your head because . . .
I'm a head-louse."

William's face
lit up.

"A talking nit?" he
said. "Wow! Just wait
till I tell Gregory!"

It wasn't until after school that William
had the chance to tell Gregory about me.
And Lizzy, too; we all agreed that it was
only fair to let her in on the secret.

Gregory was going to tea at William's
house that evening; and Lizzy lived in the
same street, so her mum said she could
come, too. At first, neither Gregory nor
Lizzy believed William when he told them
that he had met a talking head-louse – or
nit, as he kept saying – but finally he got

them to touch heads with him, and then I crawled from head to head speaking to each of them.

"Wow!" they kept saying. "*Wow!*"

We had a great time together. First we watched a bit of television – which I found interesting for about five minutes, but then it got pretty boring. It was all full of people showing off. Then I said I wanted to hear a story, so we went to William's room to look at his books.

He had *hundreds*!

Not *Treasure Island*, though. None of my new friends had a copy – which was a real shame, because I'd been thinking about it all day. I really wanted to know what happened to Jim Hawkins when he sailed away to sea.

"Cheer up!" William said. "If you like *Treasure Island*, you're going to love this!" He reached up to the highest shelf and brought down an amazing book.

It was an information book, full of facts about the sea. Right in the middle was a huge photograph of an old-fashioned sailing ship.

"There you are," said William. "That's the sort of ship Jim Hawkins went to Treasure Island on."

It was beautiful. Everything I'd imagined, and more. I could almost hear the flapping of the sails, the creak of the rigging, the splashing of the cool salt spray on the prow as it cut through the blue sea. I gazed at it, unable to speak for a moment. Then I whispered, "One day, I'm going to go on one of those . . ."

Lizzy found one of her favourite books on the shelf where William kept his scary stories, and read a bit to us. It was called *Invasion of the Brain-Suckers*. It was about a girl who discovers that her town has been invaded by little aliens who creep into people's ears, suck their brains out and turn them into zombie mind-slaves.

I didn't think it was terribly scary, to be honest. A story about people being chased by giant combs, now that would be really frightening.

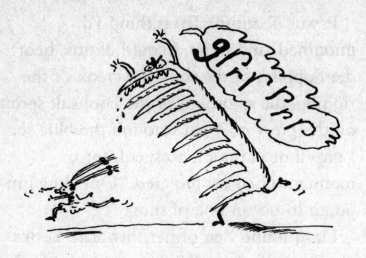

Anyway, once we'd had a couple of chapters, it was time for Gregory and Lizzy to go home. But just before they did, Gregory made a suggestion.

"You should have a name," he said to me.

Head-lice don't usually have names. But then head-lice don't usually make friends with the people they live on, and the children decided they couldn't just call me 'the louse'.

"What about 'Lenny the Louse'?"

William said with a chuckle. "Or . . . or 'Ed Louse the head-louse'!"

"Don't be silly!" Lizzy told him. He was beginning to get the giggles.

"No – no – I've got it!" William snorted, ignoring her. "What about . . . *Robert Lousey Stevenson!*" And he collapsed onto the bed, helpless with laughter.

Gregory and Lizzy looked at him scornfully.

"William," Gregory said, "this is important. Making silly jokes isn't very helpful. I think you should be more serious."

"Hold on," I said. I was sitting on Gregory's head at the time, so he heard me clearly. "He's just given me an idea. Robert Louis Stevenson wrote *Treasure Island* – about Jim Hawkins. Jim. That's it. I want to be called Jim."

It was perfect. Jim Hawkins was a boy who had extraordinary adventures. And now Jim Head-Louse was a louse who was doing extraordinary things. Once I'd said it, everyone agreed it was the only name for me.

I stayed with Gregory that night. He'd been a little scared by *Invasion of the Brain-Suckers*, and said he'd feel better if I kept him company. As he turned out the light, I whispered, "Goodnight, Gregory."

He answered softly, "'Night, Jim."

It felt good to have a name.

I waited until he was asleep, and then had one more feed; and as I did so my head was filled with wonderful, magical dreams and I too fell asleep.

Chapter Five

A Lousy Group of Friends

It was Gregory who worked it out.

I was a really special head-louse – but not because I could listen and run and jump and talk. Quite the reverse – it was because I was special that I could do all those things.

Whatever was most important to or about someone – whatever was truly *in their blood* – was passed on to me when I fed on them. Gregory's listening, William's talking, Lizzy's running and jumping and sheer, pure energy – now I shared them all.

I had friends, too: Gregory and Lizzy and William. And I had a name.

There was only one problem with our friendship.

"It's a shame Jim's so small," Lizzy said the next morning.

"It would be nice to be able to see him – properly, I mean, instead of him just looking like a little white dot."

"And if we could all hear him at once," Gregory added, "instead of him talking just to one of us, and that one telling the rest of us what he's saying."

I agreed with that – especially when I was on William's head. William was a great talker, but he wasn't much of a listener, which meant that things I wanted to say just didn't get heard sometimes.

Listen!

Then Gregory had a brainwave.

"If he feeds on someone big," he said, "then maybe he'll get big, too!"

It was a great idea. But who?

"Duncan, of course," said Lizzy. "He's the biggest in the class, by a long way."

"Yes, but he's not *huge*," said Gregory, "and anyway, it's being mean to everyone that's in *his* blood, I reckon. It'd be horrible if Jim sucked his blood and went all nasty!"

"It'd be great if Jim sucked *all* his blood, though!" said William, and everyone laughed again.

"Maybe if he can get really big, he will!" Lizzy grinned. "But who do we know who's really *really* big?"

"Yeah," William agreed, "someone who's more big than they are anything else! You know, like when people talk about them they always say, 'he's really big, isn't he?'"

"What, like Mr Little?" suggested Gregory.

There was a pause.

"But he's a *teacher*!" William squeaked. "We can't go giving a teacher nits!"

"Who said anything about giving him nits?" Gregory asked. "We'll just be *lending* him a nit."

"I'm *not* a nit, I'm a *head-louse*!" I said, but nobody heard me.

"That should work," said Lizzy. "Mr Little's probably the biggest man in the world!"

"Well, not the *whole* world," said Gregory, "but he's pretty enormous. The only problem is – how do we get Jim all the way up onto his head? He won't be able to jump *that* high!"

"We need a plan," Lizzy announced. "A very clever plan."

Which is why, just a few minutes later, William, Lizzy and Gregory were knocking on the staff-room door and asking for Mr Little.

Mr Little was huge. He
actually had to duck
to get through the
door without
banging his head.

"Excuse me,
sir," William said,
"but we were
wondering if we
could measure
your head."

"Measure my
head?" said Mr
Little, surprised.
"Whatever for?"

"It's . . . it's for a graph,"
Lizzy said. "We're doing a graph of head
sizes."

I had no idea what a graph was, but Mr
Little was obviously used to being asked to
do all sorts of strange things for them,
because without any more questions he

49

bent down and let Gregory put a string round his head.

I leaped and grabbed.

As quick as I could, I got out my little mouth-parts, bit and sucked.

Wow! Even as I fed, I could feel myself growing. It was an amazing feeling.

But while I was still feeding, Mr Little stood up straight again.

"OK?" he said.

"Er . . . could we do it again, sir?" Lizzy asked. "Just to check, you know?"

Mr Little laughed, a big loud booming chuckle. "Lizzy," he said, "I'm sure you did it right first time. Anyway, my coffee's getting cold. Out you go, now." He turned to go back into the staff-room.

"Wait! Sir! We forgot something!" Gregory said.

Mr Little sighed and turned around again.

"What is it, Gregory?" he asked.

"We forgot . . . we forgot to say thank you!" Gregory said.

"Oh, yes, thank you, Mr Little," the others all chorused, crowding round him as closely as they could.

I took my chance and leaped. It was a long way down.

Jim →

Chapter Six

Have a Lice Day

Down I fell towards the nearest head of hair – Gregory's – and landed with a muffled thump. I lay still until the staff-room door closed behind Mr Little.

"That was close!" I gasped, and sat up.

you are huge! Just like me...

William and Lizzy stared at me.

"Jim!" William gasped. "I can see you! You're *huge*! You're as big as a . . . a ladybird or something!"

"And we can hear you, too! It worked!" Lizzy said, jumping up and down with excitement.

The staff-room door opened again.

"Out!" Mr Little bellowed.

We ran.

Or at least, the children ran; I clung tight to Gregory's hair. Out of the door we crashed, all of us laughing, and hurtled across the playground. We ran, we raced, we rocketed.

And we tripped. That is, Gregory tripped, a great crashing fall that shook us both as he hit the hard playground.

"Watch out, Eggy Greggy!" Duncan sneered. "You tripped over my foot! Say sorry!"

Gregory picked himself up, slowly and painfully.

"You did that on purpose, Duncan!" he said angrily.

"Oh, listen," Duncan taunted him. "Eggy Greggy's going to cry! Boo hoo!"

"Leave him alone, you big bully!"
William shouted. Duncan reached out and
pushed him in the face, so hard he sat
down with a bump on the ground. Then
he pushed Lizzy as well.

I felt furious. Just because he was bigger
than them, this ugly monster was hurting
my friends. But what could I do? I was
only a head-louse – a big one now, but
still tiny compared to Duncan.

"Right, Eggy Greggy," Duncan went
on, grabbing Gregory by the hair. "You
know why I call you Eggy Greggy, don't

you? It's because your hair's full of nits'
eggs. And if we're not careful, we'll all
catch nits off you. So I'm going to do us
all a favour, and give your stinky hair a
good washing – in the toilet! Come on!"

He started to drag Gregory away.

I could have leaped to safety on
someone else's head. But suddenly I knew
I had to do something – or at least I had
to try. Even if horrid old Duncan squashed
me flat, I couldn't let him hurt my friends
and not do my best to stop him.

"Leave him alone!" I shouted, standing
up as tall as I could.

Duncan looked round, unsure of where
the voice had come from. "Who said
that?" he demanded.

"I did!" I yelled at him. "Down here!
Just by your ugly great fingers!"

Duncan looked down at his hand.

"No," I said, "the *other* ugly great
fingers!"

This time, he looked at the hand gripping Gregory's hair. "Eeeeugh!" he went, letting go. "What *is* it?" He peered closer. "It's a nit! Eeeeugh! Eeeeugh! I *told* you he was covered in nits' eggs!"

"A nit *is* an egg, you imbecile!" I told him. "I'm a head-louse!"

He leaped back. "It's talking!" he yelped. Then he peered at me again. "Wait a minute," he said suspiciously. "Nits aren't supposed to be this big!"

"*Head-lice*, you fool!" I snapped.

He jumped back again. He was starting to look a little nervous – and suddenly I had an idea.

"But you're right," I went on, "none of your Earth-lice are as big as me."

"*Earth*-lice?" he said. "Are you trying to tell me you come from . . . from . . . outer space?"

"How else do you explain a giant talking head-louse?" I asked him. "Especially one that can suck out the brains of humans and turn you into my slaves!" Then I shouted out, "Capture him, slaves! I feel a bit hungry! I know he hasn't got much of a brain, but it should keep me going till lunchtime!"

Lizzy was the first one to realize what I wanted them to do. After all, she was the one who'd read us *Invasion of the Brain-Suckers*. She widened her eyes into the horrible blank stare of a zombie mind-slave. Then, holding her hands like claws and raising them at Duncan, she lurched forward. Gregory and William gaped for a moment. Then, suddenly, they got the idea, and did the same. William made a low moaning sound.

Duncan backed away nervously.

"Hang on . . . you're joking, right? You're not really going to suck out my brain, are you?" He looked around wildly from one to another of my friends. "William? Lizzy? Gregory? This is a joke, isn't it?"

"I never joke!" I thundered. "Surrender! Come close so that we may eat your brain!"

Gregory took another lurching step forward, and made a weird hissing noise.

This was too much for Duncan.

"Aaaaaaaaaaggggggh!!!" he screamed, running away. "I'll tell! I'll tell! I'll tell!"

Suddenly, there was silence. All over the whole playground, all the games and noise and chatter stopped. Everyone stared in amazement. Duncan, who made everyone's lives a misery, was running away, screaming, from quiet little Gregory – and threatening to tell!

Duncan, hearing all the playground noise stop at once, halted and stood paralysed with fear. He looked frantically around. Every face was staring at him. The only movement was from Gregory, still lurching towards him in that stiff zombie-like walk.

You could almost see the thought spreading across the playground, as everyone remembered all the mean things Duncan had ever done to them. You could almost hear the children thinking, *If*

Gregory can scare Duncan like this – maybe I can, too!

One by one, all the other children in the playground stuck out their arms, and like silent robots, they began their stiff-legged march towards the boy who had made so many playtimes a misery.

"Aaaaaaaaaaggggggggh!!!" Duncan screamed again. "Aaaaaaaaaaggggggggh!!! Aaaaaaaaaaggggggggh!!!"

And he bolted for the school door, and ran inside.

Chapter Seven

A Lousy Way to End a Story

Things were a lot more fun in school after that. Duncan was too scared to go into the playground for about a week, and even when he did go out there again he kept well away from all the other children.

He was much better in class, too. I was tempted from time to time to pop up on somebody's head and talk to him, but I thought that might be just a bit too cruel.

63

Life was great for me. Every evening I went home with either Gregory or William; and I spent most playtimes racing around on Lizzy's head. I never met the mad louse again, though. Perhaps he moved to another head – or maybe the Comb finally found his hiding place . . .

During lessons, I wandered around a bit, leaping from head to head and exploring. And feeding. Some of you were probably hoping this story would end with me becoming a vegetarian or something. Well, forget it. I'm a head-louse! I feed on human blood! I mean, I don't see you lot feeling sorry for yoghurt, do I?

We went on board.

The ship was a sort of floating museum, to show people what life was like on an old-fashioned sailing ship. The crew – explained the captain, who was showing us around – were mostly teenagers who'd just left school, and they were having the time of their lives. For the last few weeks they'd been sailing around the country, showing the ship to schoolchildren and other visitors, and now they were preparing to go on a long voyage and really learn how to sail the ship properly.

Gregory put his hand up. "Excuse me," he said, "but will it be a voyage like in *Treasure Island*?"

The captain nodded.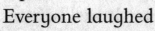
"Just like *Treasure Island*, young man," he said, "except without the pirates, I hope!"

Everyone laughed – except Gregory and me. He knew what I was thinking.

"You want to go, don't you, Jim?" he asked later, when we were up on deck having a look round.

"Yes," I told him. "Yes, I really do!"

"I think you should," he said quietly. "Let's tell William and Lizzy."

William wasn't happy about the idea. In fact, he nearly burst into tears. "Jim *can't* go!" he said. "He *can't*!"

"No, he *has* to," said Lizzy. "Don't you

see? Ever since that first day, he's loved *Treasure Island*! Remember when you showed him the picture of the sailing ship? This could be his only chance to sail on one! We *can't* stop him, William; it wouldn't be fair!"

"Anyway," Gregory added, "he'll come back. Won't you, Jim?"

"Of course!" I told them. "The captain said the ship would be back well before Christmas!"

"But how will you find your way back to *us*?" William insisted. "You don't know how to read maps!"

"He'll feed on the navigator, of course!" Gregory said, and we all laughed – a little sadly, because they were going to miss me, and I them. Then I leaped from head to head, telling each of them how much I loved them and what good friends they'd been to me, and promising to come back as soon as I could. And they told me how

much they would miss me, and promised
to think of me every day. And we all said
goodbye.

"Come on," Lizzy said, "before we
change our minds!"

She marched up to a passing crew-
member – a tall, skinny boy with red hair
– and said to him,

"Excuse me . . . but we're
doing a graph on head
sizes. Could you bend
down so that we can
measure your
head?"

Jim

So it was that the next morning I found myself high in the rigging, as we set sail for far-away seas. The sun glittered and shone on the sparkling water, the great sails billowed in the wind, the land drifted away behind us.

I felt just like Jim Hawkins.

I missed my friends, but I was so excited about the adventure that lay ahead. I leaped from sailor to sailor experiencing everything that I could, seeing how the whole ship ran. Then, at the end of the first day, I returned to the red-haired crew-member.

"Can we put the light out soon?" asked one of his crew-mates from his bunk.

"In a minute," the red-haired sailor answered, getting into bed. "I can't get to sleep unless I read just a little bit first. And I'm really looking forward to this one –

it'll be just right for the voyage." He settled down in his bunk, took a book out from under his pillow – and my happiness was complete.

It was *Treasure Island*.

He turned to Chapter One, and we began to read.

The End